Sweet Dreams Stories

Written by
Jillian Harker

Illustrated by
Andy Everitt-Stewart
Louise Garner, Julie Nicholson
and Pamela Venus

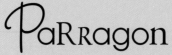

Bath · New York · Singapore · Hong Kong · Cologne · Delhi
Melbourne · Amsterdam · Johannesburg · Auckland · Shenzhen

Contents

No One Like You   6

If You Hold My Hand 34

Just as Well, Really!   62

On my Own   90

Guess what I Want? 118

A Goodnight Kiss   146

Kiss it Better   174

Lost and Alone   202

No One Like You

Ruff was hungry. A huge grumble rumbled
round his tummy. He could hear Rufus clattering
round in the kitchen. A delicious smell of freshly
baked cakes sailed past his nose.
"Yummy," thought Ruff.

9

Ruff skipped into the kitchen – Rufus was tidying up.
"Would you like some help?" asked Ruff. "I could try
one of those cakes for you."

"Oh, really!" said Rufus, smiling.

11

"No one makes cakes like you," said Ruff.

13

Ruff was bored. He twiddled his fingers, tapped his toes and twiddled his fingers again. He had no one to play with.

Later, Ruff tip-toed back into the living room—
Rufus was reading.

"Would you like something better to read?"
asked Ruff. "I could find you an exciting story."

"Oh, really!" said Rufus, smiling.

"No one tells a story like you," said Ruff.

Ruff was fed up. He was trying to make a model car. He fiddled and twiddled and fiddled, but he couldn't put it together.
Then he had an idea!

21

Ruff galloped into the garden—Rufus was digging.

"Would you like something fun to do?" asked Ruff. "I could let you help me with my model car."

"Oh, really!" said Rufus, smiling.

23

"No one's as much fun as you,"
said Ruff.

24

It was bedtime! Rufus tucked Ruff into bed. Ruff was feeling scared. He didn't like the shadows that flickered all round – it was very quiet.

Then he had an idea!

Ruff crept out of his bedroom and into Rufus' room.

Rufus was snoring loudly. It made Ruff giggle and woke Rufus up.

"Would you like someone to cuddle?" asked Ruff. "I'm very good at cuddling."

"Oh, really!" said Rufus, smiling.

"No one cuddles like you,"

yawned Ruff, climbing into
Rufus' bed.

31

"Oh, really!" said Rufus...

32

"Well, no one loves you as much as I do, because there's no one like you."

33

If You Hold My Hand

Oakey's mum opened the front door. "Come on, Oakey. Let's go outside and explore."

ROSE COTTAGE

But Oakey wasn't really sure. He was only small, and the world looked big and scary. 37

"Only if you promise to hold my hand," said Oakey.

So Oakey's mum led him down the long lane.
Oakey wished he was back at home again!

"This looks like a great place to play. Shall we take a look? What do you say?" asked Oakey's mum.

"Only if you hold my hand," said Oakey.

And Oakey did it!

"Look at me! I can do it!" he cried.

"This slide looks fun. Would you like to try?" asked Oakey's mum.

Oakey looked at the ladder. It **stretched** right up to the sky.

44

"I'm only small," said Oakey. "I don't know if I can climb that high — *unless you hold my hand.*"

45

And Oakey did i

"Wheee! Did you see me?" he cried.

47

"We'll take a short cut through the wood," said Oakey's mum.

'I'm not sure if we should," said Oakey.
'It looks dark in there. Well, I suppose we could –
will you hold my hand?'

49

And Oakey did it!

"Boo! I scared you!" he cried.

Deep in the woo•
Oakey found a
stream, shaded
by beautiful
tall trees.

"Stepping stones, look!"
said Oakey's mum.
"Do you think you could jump
across these?"

"Maybe," said
Oakey. "*I just need you
to hold my hand, please.*"

53

And Oakey did it!

One...

two.

three...

four...

"Your turn now, Mum," cried Oakey,
holding out his hand.

Beyond the wood, Oakey and his mum
ran up the hill, and all the way
down to the sea.

"Come on, Oakey," called his mum.

"Would you like to paddle in the sea with me?"

57

But the sea looked big, and he was only small.

Suddenly, Oakey knew that didn't matter at all. He turned to his mum and smiled...

"I can do **anything** if you hold my hand," he said.

Just as Well, Really!

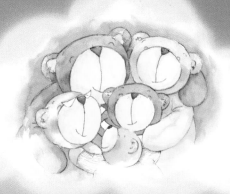

Rumpus liked water.

He liked the
drippiness and
droppiness,

the **splashiness**
and sloppiness
of it!

He liked it so much that, whenever there
was water around...

...Rumpus somehow always managed to–

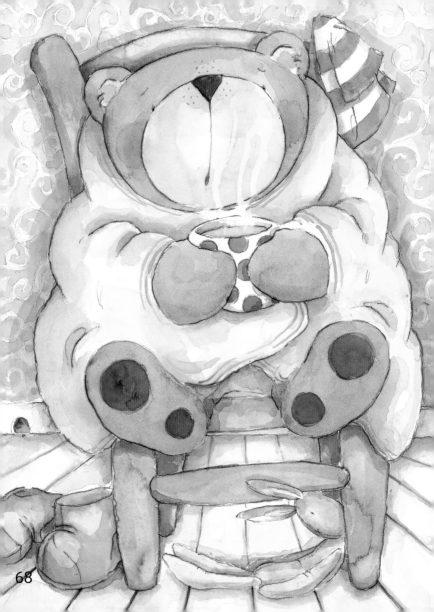

But Mum loved Rumpus, so

ery time, she simply sighed–and she mopped up the mess.

69

Rumpus loved mud.

He loved the way you could

plodge

in it,

splodge
in it,
slide
in it and
glide
in it!

He loved it so much that, whenever
there was mud around...

...Rumpus somehow always managed to—

But Dad loved Rumpus, so

every time, he simply sighed – and
he sponged off the splatters.

Rumpus enjoyed paint.

He liked to
splatter
and
dash it,

to spread
and
splash
it!

He enjoyed it so much that, whenever there was paint around...

But Rumpus' brother loved him, so

very time, he simply sighed—and cleaned himself up.

Rumpus liked to find out how things worked.

He loved the prodding and probing,

the **wiggling** and the **jiggling,** the unscrewing and the undoing!

loved it so much that, whenever Rumpus was around...

...things didn't work for long!

84

85

But Granny loved Rumpus,
so she simply sighed – and
she tidied away the clutter.

Rumpus loved his mum, dad...

brother and granny...

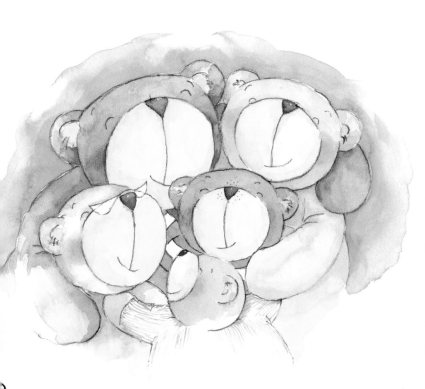

Rumpus' mum, dad, brother and granny loved Rumpus...

...just as well, really!

On my Own

Deep in the jungle, where only wild things
go, Mungo's mum was teaching him
what a young monkey needs to know.
"Some things just aren't safe to try alone,"
she said.

"Why not?" said Mungo. "I'm big
enough to do things—
on my own!"

93

"Now Mungo,"

said Mum, "listen carefully, please. We're going to go through these trees. Stay close to me, and hold my hand. Did you hear what I said?

Do you understand?"

"It's okay, Mum. I won't slip or fall. I can swing across there with no trouble at all," said Mungo. "I'm big enough to do it—
on my own!" And off he swung

And did Mungo hear poor old Snake groan?

No!
Mungo just laughed.
"I told you I could do it
on my own."

"Now, we're going to cross the river using these stones," said Mum. "But, Mungo, I'd rather you didn't do this alone."

"But Mum," said Mungo, and he ran on without stopping, "I'm really good at jumping and hopping. I'm big enough to do it—

on my own!"

And off he sprang!

103

"That Mungo trampled on my nose!" said Croc.

"Next time, I'll nibble off his toes!"
And did Mungo hear poor old Croc groan?
No! Mungo just smiled. "I told you I could do
on my own."

"**Mungo,**" said Mum, with a serious look on her face, "the jungle can be a dangerous place. There are all sorts of corners for creatures to hide, so, from here on, make sure that you stay by my side."

107

"Oh, Mum," said Mungo, "I don't need to wait for you. I can easily find my own way through. I'm big enough to do it– on my own!"

Lion rubbed the lump on his nose.

"Ouch!

That Mungo's so careless!" he said.

And did Mungo hear poor old Lion groan?

No! Mungo just grinned. "I told you I could do it

on my own."

"I think I've had quite enough for one day," Mum said. "So off you go, little monkey! Now it really is time for bed!"

It was Mungo's turn to let out a **groan**.
"I don't want to go to bed –
on my own!"
"Don't worry," said Mum. "Come on,
kiss me goodnight, and I promise I'll
hold you and cuddle you tight."

114

Lion roared, "Is that Mungo still awake?"

"Yes!" snapped Crocodile.

116

"Lets help him go to sleep," hissed Snake.

And into the velvety, starry sky drifted the sounds of a jungle lullaby.

117

Guess What I Want?

"Guess what I want?" said Ruff to Rufus.

"Something from me?" asked Rufus.
"Now, let me see – what could it be?"
"You've got to guess,"
said Ruff.

p.vénus
121

"You want me to tie a string to the moon, so you can pull it around like a giant balloon?" said Rufus.

"We could tie the moon
to the post of your bed,
to shine through the night
above your head."

124

125

"Would you really get me the moon?" asked Ruff.

"Well, it would be quite hard to climb up that high, but for you, of course, I'd give it a try," said Rufus.

"Guess again," laughed Ruff.

127

"You want me to catch you
a shining white star,
and capture its bright light
for you in a jar?"
said Rufus.

128

"It would twinkle all night and light up your dreams, and dance round your room, mixed with yellow moonbe

131

"Would you really fetch me a star?" asked Ruff.

"Well, catching a star isn't easy to do, but I'd give it a try, because I love you," said Rufus.

"Guess again," laughed Ruff.

133

"You want me to capture the song of the breeze, as it lulls its way gently through leaves on the trees," said Rufus.

"You'd be able to turn on the breeze's soft tune
for the starlight to dance along with the moon."

"Would you really bring me
the song of the breeze?" asked Ruff.

"Well, the breeze moves so fast, it isn't
easy to do, but I'd find a way to do it
for you," said Rufus.

Ruff thought hard.

"To tie down the moon, wouldn't be right. And the sky is the place to leave the starlight. It wouldn't be fair to stop the wind's song. Now, try one more guess—your first three were wrong!"

141

"I know. I was teasin
I think you want this

142

143

...a huge great big cuddle, and a lovely big kiss!"

145

A Goodnight Kiss

"It's bedtime now, Oakey," said Mum.

148

Oakey curled up in the chair.
His ears began to droop and he muttered,
"Oh, that's not fair!"

"Have a drink first," smiled Mum, "then you must go.
Five minutes more!" begged Oakey
Mum answered, "No!"

150

Oakey's ears drooped and off he went.
But he was **back in a flash!**

"Where's your drink?" asked Mum.
"You haven't been very long.
You look scared, Oakey.
Is there something wrong?"

"There's a monster
in the kitchen,
with long, white shaggy hair,
lurking in the corner,
behind the rocking chair,"
said Oakey.

153

Mum laughed.
"Oh, Oakey, you've made
a mistake.
That's no monster. It's a
mop." And she gave the m[op]
a shake.

154

Oakey's ears drooped
and off he went.
But he was
back in a flash!

"What's the matter?"
asked Mum.

"There's a ghost
in the hallway, hovering around.
Look, there it is floating
just above the ground,"
he wailed.

"Oh, Oakey, you've made a mistake.
That's no ghost.
It's just an old coat, hanging on
the hook.
Coats don't float!" laughed Mum.

Oakey's ears drooped and
off he went.
But he was
back in a flash!

"Why aren't you in bed, Oakey?"
asked Mum.

"There's a
great big lump
beneath the sheets.
It's waiting to get me.
I'm scared it's going
to pounce. Please come
and see," sniffed Oakey.

161

"Oh, Oakey, you've made a mistake.
The only thing underneath the sheets,
is your old teddy bear," smiled Mum.

Oakey's ears drooped
and he got into bed.
But he didn't
close his eyes.

"Why aren't you asleep?"
asked Mum.

"There are
huge creepy crawlies
underneath my bed.
And I can't get the thought of them
out of my head,"
complained Oakey.

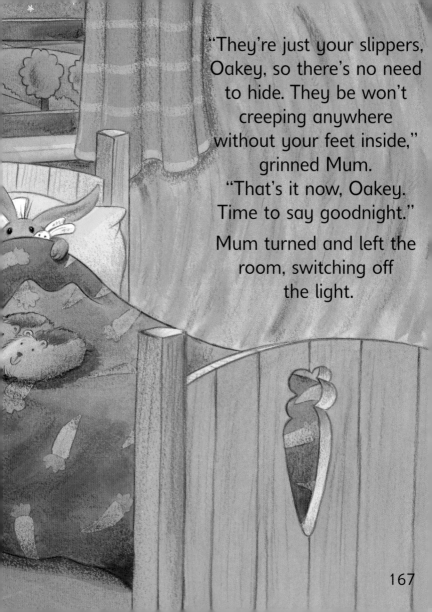

"They're just your slippers, Oakey, so there's no need to hide. They be won't creeping anywhere without your feet inside," grinned Mum.

"That's it now, Oakey. Time to say goodnight."

Mum turned and left the room, switching off the light.

And then Oakey saw it,
standing by the door.
The monster!

It moved across the floor and walked
straight towards him, with its arms
stretched out. Oakey's mouth opened,
but he found he couldn't shout.

The monster leaned over him and Oakey closed his eyes. What happened next gave Oakey an enormous surprise. The monster picked him up and cuddled him tight. Monsters just don't do that.

This couldn't be right!

Then Mum's voice whispered,
"Don't worry, it's just me.
When I said 'Goodnight' just now,
I forgot to give you this."

Then 'Monster Mum' gave Oakey
a goodnight kiss!

Kiss it Better

Rumpus was romping around the living room.
He cartwheeled across the carpet.

He turned a somersault on the sofa.

"Be careful!"
called Mum.

Too late! Rumpus slipped from the sofa, crumpled onto the carpet and banged his head on the floor.

"Come here and I'll kiss it better," said Mum.

She hugged Rumpus and planted a kiss on his forehead.

"Now, go and find something less rowdy to do," she said.

Rumpus rushed out into the garden
and began to ride his bike.
Round and round he raced.

"Watch out!"
called Mum.

Too late!
Rumpus crashed into
the corner of the
wheelbarrow...

and tumbled to the
ground and grazed his knee.

"My leg hurts!"

he wailed. 185

"Come here and I'll *kiss it better*," said Mu

She hugged Rumpus and planted a kiss on his knee.

"Now, go and find something safer to do," she said.

Rumpus ran up the grassy slope.

Then he rolled down.
"Roly poly, down the hill," he sang.

"Look where you're going!"
called Mum.

Too late!

Rumpus rolled right into
the rose bush.
The thorns scratched him all
along his arm.

"My arm's sore!"
cried Rumpus.

"Come here and I'll **kiss it better**", said Mum and she planted kisses all up his arm.

"Now, try and keep out of trouble," she said.

Mum went into the kitchen.
"I need a break,"
she thought.

194

She made a cup of tea.
She cut herself a slice of cake.
Then, she sat down for five minutes.

Just as she picked up her cup,
Rumpus zoomed into the kitchen...

on his skateboard.

"Rumpus!" said Mum.
"Can't you find something more sensible to do?"

197

Mum moved into the living room.
"I need a rest," she thought.
She sat down on the sofa and picked
up the paper.

"Boom!
Boom!
Boom!"

In marched Rumpus,
banging on his drum.
Mum sighed a loud sigh.

199

"Is anything wrong?" asked Rumpus.

"I've got a headache!" said Mum.

"Never mind," smiled
Rumpus, throwing his
arms round her.
"I'll soon
kiss it better."

Lost and Alone

Deep in the jungle, Mungo was trying to slip off through the trees.

"Mungo, tell me where you're going, please," called Mum.

"What are you planning to do today?"

"I'm just going to play," smiled Mungo.
"Okay," said Mum.
"But no monkey business!"

Elephant was enjoying a peaceful drink when Mungo crept up and yelled, "Hi, Elephant!

Want to play?"

Then he added, "I know a good game.'

"Funny faces!" said Mungo.
"What do you say?"
"I'm not sure," said Elephant.
"I don't know how to play."

"**Easy**" said Mungo. "All you have to do, is pull a funny face. Look, I'll show you."

And he took hold of Elephant's trunk.

Mungo wound Elephant's trunk round and round
and slipped the end through.
He pulled it into a knot.

"Wow, Elephant!" he giggled.

"What a funny face you've got!"

"Hey!" gurgled Elephant. "How do I get out
of this?"

But Mungo was gone!

Down by the river bank,
Crocodile was trying to nap,
when Mungo jumped out of the trees,
and gave his nose a tap.

"Want to play?" Mungo asked.

"I know a good game."

Really?" said Crocodile,
suspiciously.
"What's its name?"

213

"Funny Faces," said Mungo.
"What do you say?"
"I'm not sure," said Crocodile.
"I don't know how to play."

"**Easy,**" said Mungo. "All you have to do, is pull a funny face. Look, I'll show you." And he took hold of Crocodile's jaws.

215

Mungo pulled on one jaw, and pushed on the other.
Then he jammed them both together.

"Hey, Croc!" he giggled.
"That's a really funny face!"
"Help!" choked Crocodile.

"How do I get out of this?"
But Mungo was gone!

Lion was trying to have a laze in the sun, when Mungo swung down and asked, **"Want some fun?"** Then he added, "Come on. I know a good game."

"Yeah?" said Lion, suspiciously. "What's its name?"

"Funny Faces,"
said Mungo.
"What do
you say?"
"I'm not sure," said Lion.
"I don't know how to play."

"Easy," said Mungo.
"All you have to do, is pull a
funny face. Look, I'll show you."

And he took hold of
Lion's bottom lip.

221

Mungo pulled the lip up over Lion's nose.
"You see," he said, "that's the way it goes."

Then he ran off, smiling, through the trees.
"Forget what Mum said," thought Mungo.
"I'll do as I please."
He swung through the branches, but, after a while,
Mungo's face lost its smile.
"I don't know where I am!" he wailed.

"That's a funny face," said Elephant.
"He wins the game for sure."
"You're right," laughed Lion.
"Come on, Mungo, give us more."

"Well, shall we help him?" Lion roared.
"What do you think?"

"I'm not sure," said Elephant.
"He did disturb my drink."

"And he woke me up," Crocodile complained,
"which really wasn't fun."

"He wrecked my rest, too," Lion said.
"You're not the only one."

227

"If we agree to help, Mungo,"
he animals all said. "Then no more funny faces.
Can you get that into your head?"

Mungo looked much happier than he'd
done in quite a while.
"No more tricks!" Mungo promised,
and he thanked each of the three.

"Being lost and alone
wasn't any fun for me!"

Created by The Complete Works

This edition published by Parragon in 2010

Parragon
Queen Street House
4 Queen Street
Bath BA1 1HE, UK

ISBN 978-1-4454-0465-3

Printed in China